THE ROMANCE SCAM

Mike Nash

Copyright © 2024 by Mike Nash

All rights reserved.

No portion of this book may be reproduced in any form without written permission from the publisher or author, except as permitted by U.S. copyright law.

ACKNOWLEDGMENTS

Writing this book has been a deeply personal journey, and I am profoundly grateful to everyone who has supported me along the way. To my family, especially my children, Brighton, Vanessa and Helen, your unwavering love and patience have been my strength. To my friends and colleagues, your encouragement and understanding have meant the world to me during this challenging time.

A special thanks to the *Catfished* YouTube channel for creating the impactful video that inspired this book. This is a true story, shared by a woman known as Jillian, who courageously sent an email to the *Catfished* channel, detailing her heartbreaking experience. Your dedication to exposing the realities of online scams is truly commendable, and I also want to extend my deepest sympathies to Jillian—I'm sorry for the pain you've endured, and I hope that sharing your story will help others avoid similar heartache.

Finally, to the readers, thank you for taking the time to engage with this story. My hope is that this book serves as a source of insight and helps raise awareness about the dangers of online scams.

DEDICATION

To everyone who has been affected by romance scams, especially Jillian, whose story is told within these pages. This book is for you. Your strength in the face of deception and your courage to rebuild after heartbreak is a testament to the resilience of the human spirit. May your journey through these difficult experiences lead you to healing, justice, and a renewed belief in the power of genuine love and trust.

Contents

1. The Lonely Heart — 1
2. The Perfect Gentleman — 7
3. The Web of Lies — 13
4. The Unraveling — 17
5. The Investigation Begins — 23
6. The Web Unravels — 29
7. The Fallout — 33
8. The Legal Battle — 39
9. A New Beginning — 44
10. Moving Forward — 49
11. About the Author — 52

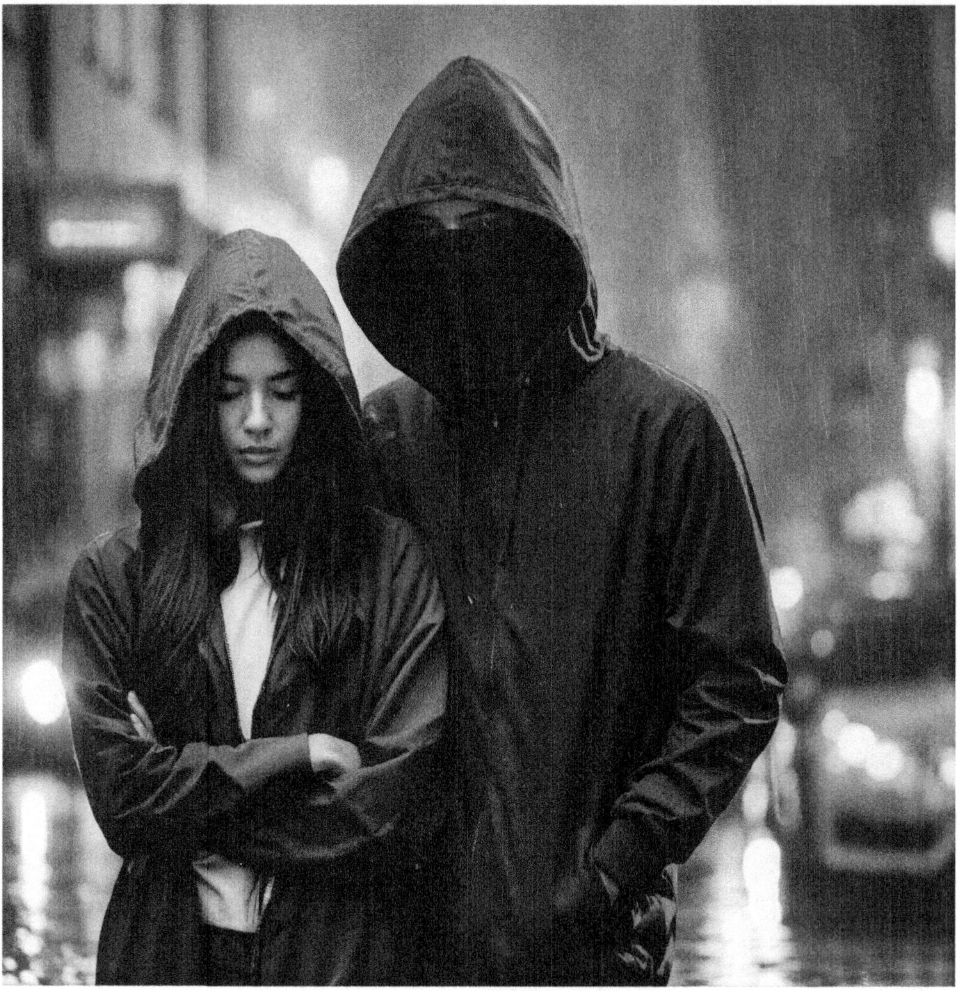

Chapter One

The Lonely Heart

Jillian Parker was the kind of woman who had spent her life giving everything she had to others, leaving little for herself. At 42, she was a single mother of two teenagers, Ethan and Megan, and worked tirelessly in the human services department of her local government. Her days were filled with the demands of helping others—coordinating resources for those in need, managing cases of domestic abuse, and ensuring that the vulnerable in her community were cared for. It was a job she was passionate about, but it left her emotionally drained and with very little time for herself.

Her evenings were a blur of homework help, cooking dinner, and trying to maintain some semblance of order in a household where the chaos of adolescence reigned supreme. Ethan, 16, was in that difficult phase of trying to assert his independence while still needing his mother's guidance. Megan, 14, was navigating the treacherous waters of early teenagehood, dealing with peer pressure, body image issues, and the rollercoaster of emotions that came with growing up. Jillian did her best to be there for them, to listen, to support, and to guide, but it was exhausting. By the time she finally had a moment to herself, she was too tired to do anything but collapse into bed.

The loneliness crept in during those late-night hours when the house was quiet, and there was no one to talk to. She would lie in bed, staring at the ceiling, feeling the weight of her solitude. It wasn't that she didn't love her children—she did, more than anything—but she missed having someone to share her life with. Someone who would hold her at the end of a long day, listen to her thoughts, and tell her that everything would be okay. The loneliness was a constant, nagging presence that she tried to ignore, but it was always there, lurking in the background of her busy life.

One evening, after a particularly grueling day at work and a heated argument with Ethan about his grades, Jillian found herself scrolling aimlessly through her phone. She had heard about online dating from friends and colleagues, but had always dismissed it as something for younger people or those looking for a casual fling. But tonight, the thought of going to bed alone again, feeling that familiar ache of loneliness, was too much to bear. She opened the app store and downloaded a popular dating app, telling herself it was just to see what was out there, just to browse.

The app asked her to create a profile, and she hesitated for a moment. What would she even say about herself? It had been so long since she had thought of herself in terms of dating or romance. Eventually, she settled on something simple: "Single mom, 42, looking for companionship and a meaningful connection. I love my job in human services and my two wonderful kids. I enjoy reading, hiking, and a good cup of coffee." She uploaded a recent photo—one that Megan had taken of her on a rare family hike in the nearby mountains. In it,

Jillian was smiling, her brown hair framing her face, her eyes reflecting a contentment she didn't always feel.

After setting up her profile, she began to swipe through potential matches. There were a lot of profiles that didn't catch her interest—men posing with fish they had caught, shirtless gym selfies, or profiles filled with vague, impersonal statements. She was about to give up when she came across a profile that made her pause.

His name was Evan Nicholson, a 45-year-old military man stationed overseas. His profile picture was striking—he was dressed in uniform, a serious expression on his handsome face, with piercing blue eyes that seemed to look right through the screen. His profile was thoughtful and articulate, describing himself as a man who valued honor, loyalty, and family. He mentioned that he was a widower, that his wife had passed away several years ago, and that he was looking for someone to share his life with—a partner who understood the importance of trust and communication.

Jillian felt a flutter of excitement as she read his profile. There was something about Evan that drew her in, something that felt genuine and real. She hesitated for a moment before swiping right, wondering if a man like him would even be interested in someone like her. But she quickly brushed aside her doubts, telling herself that there was no harm in trying.

To her surprise, it didn't take long for Evan to respond. Within an hour, she received a notification that they had matched, and a message from him popped up on her screen. "Hi Jillian, it's a pleasure to meet you. I was really drawn to your profile. You seem like a wonderful person, and I'd love to get to know you better."

Jillian's heart skipped a beat as she read his message. She took a deep breath before typing a response, trying to sound casual despite the excitement bubbling up inside her. "Hi Evan, it's great to meet you too. Thank you for your kind words. I'd love to get to know you better as well."

What followed was a whirlwind of messages that left Jillian feeling like she was floating on air. Evan was charming, attentive, and genuinely interested in her life. He asked her about her work, her kids, and her hobbies, and he shared stories from his own life—his experiences in the military, his love for his late wife, and his hopes for the future. They talked about everything from their favorite books to their thoughts on raising teenagers, and Jillian found herself looking forward to their conversations more and more each day.

Evan's compliments were both flattering and thoughtful. He told her that she had beautiful eyes, that her smile was infectious, and that he admired her dedication to her work and her family. He made her feel seen, appreciated, and valued in a way she hadn't felt in a long time. The loneliness that had weighed so heavily on her began to lift, replaced by a warmth that spread through her whenever she thought about Evan.

As the days turned into weeks, their connection deepened. Evan told Jillian that he was stationed in Syria, working on a dangerous mission that required him to be away from home for long periods of time. He explained that it was difficult for him to access his accounts while he was deployed, and that he didn't have many people he could trust. Despite the distance and the challenges, he assured Jillian that he was committed to making their relationship work, and that he couldn't wait to come home and be with her.

Jillian found herself falling for Evan more and more each day. She loved the way he made her feel special, the way he seemed to understand her in a way that no one else did. She fantasized about the day they would finally meet in person, imagining how it would feel to wrap her arms around him, to feel his strong embrace, to look into his eyes and see the man she had come to care for so deeply.

But as much as she wanted to believe in their future together, there was a small voice in the back of her mind that whispered doubts. It was the voice of caution, the voice that reminded her of the stories she had heard about online dating scams, about people who preyed on the vulnerable and lonely. Jillian pushed those thoughts aside, convincing herself that Evan was different, that he was real, and that what they had was genuine.

After all, she reasoned, why would a man like Evan go to such lengths to win her trust and affection if he wasn't sincere? Why would he spend hours talking to her, sharing his life and his dreams, if he didn't truly care about her? Jillian chose to ignore the nagging doubts, allowing herself to be swept up in the romance of it all.

Little did she know that this was just the beginning of a journey that would take her down a dark and treacherous path, one that would test her in ways she never imagined. For now, though, Jillian was happy—happier than she had been in a long time—and she was willing to take the risk, to follow her heart, even if it meant stepping into the unknown.

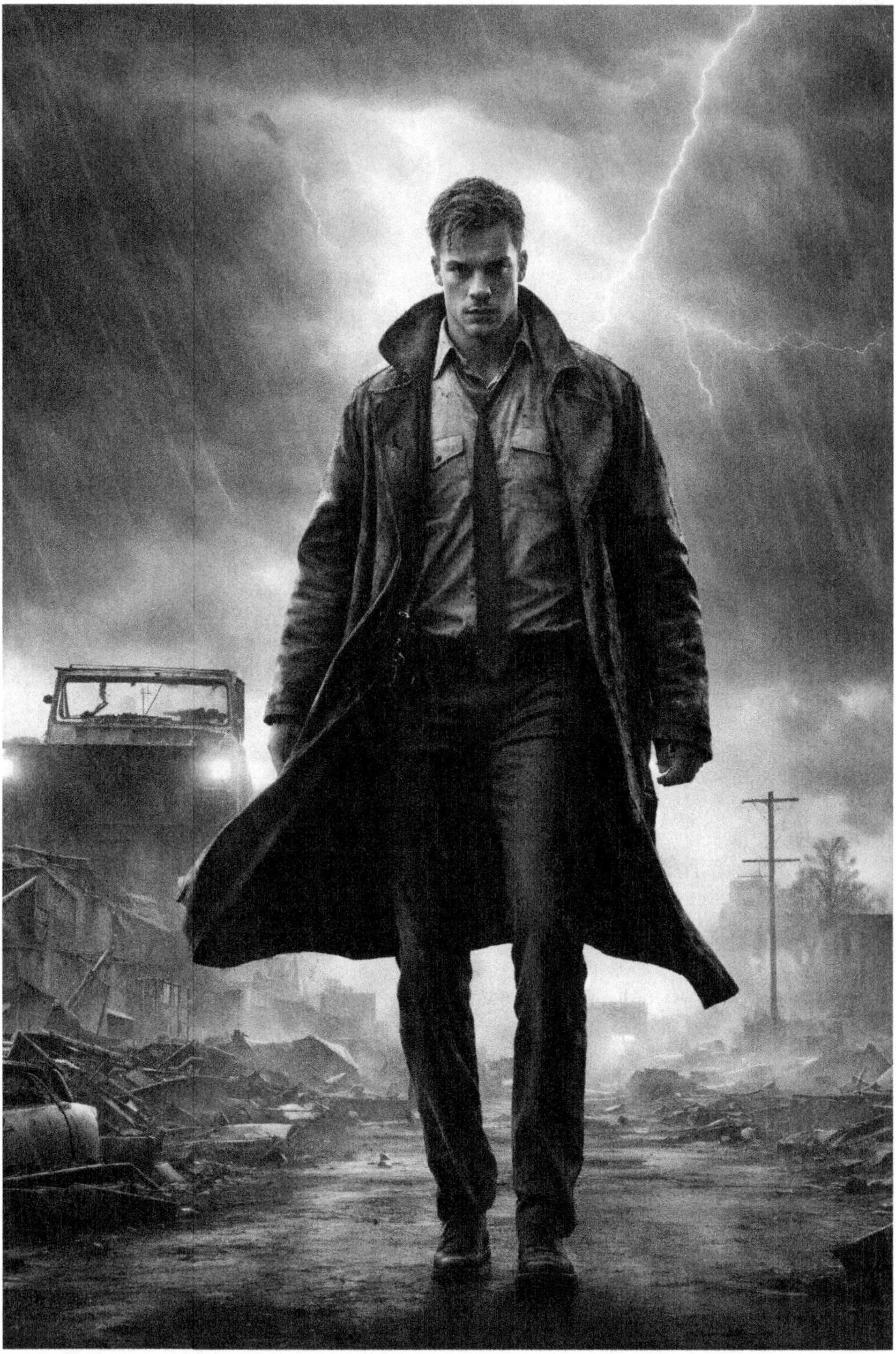

Chapter Two

The Perfect Gentleman

Days turned into weeks, and Jillian's connection with Evan only grew stronger. Every morning, she would wake up to a sweet message from him, often filled with compliments or thoughtful questions about her day ahead. His messages were like a bright spot in her otherwise stressful life. She would sneak glances at her phone during work, smiling as she read his words, feeling a warm glow inside her that she hadn't felt in years.

Evan seemed to be everything she had ever wanted in a partner—thoughtful, caring, and deeply respectful. He listened when she talked about the challenges of raising two teenagers on her own, offering words of encouragement and understanding. He would tell her stories about his own life, about the love he had for his late wife and how much he missed her. Evan was open about the pain he had endured after her passing, and how it had taken him years to even consider the possibility of loving someone else. Jillian felt honored that he was willing to share such intimate details with her, and it only deepened her feelings for him.

One evening, after a particularly difficult day at work, Jillian came home feeling completely drained. A case involving a young mother and her children had struck a chord with her, reminding her of her own struggles when her kids were younger. She felt emotionally raw, and all she wanted was to talk to Evan. She knew that he would make her feel better, that he would say just the right thing to lift her spirits.

As soon as she settled onto the couch, she opened her phone and saw that Evan had already sent her a message.

"Hey, beautiful. I was thinking about you all day. How are you holding up?"

Jillian smiled, already feeling a bit better just reading his words. She quickly typed a response.

"It's been a tough day, Evan. Work was really hard, and I'm feeling pretty drained. But it helps to hear from you."

Within moments, Evan responded.

"I'm so sorry to hear that, Jillian. I wish I could be there to hold you right now. You're such a strong woman, and I admire you so much for what you do. But remember, it's okay to let someone else take care of you sometimes."

Jillian felt a lump in her throat as she read his message. How was it possible that someone she had never even met in person could make her feel so understood, so cared for? She had been strong for so long, holding everything together for her kids, for her job, for herself. But Evan's words made her realize how much she longed to be taken care of, to let someone else shoulder the burden for a while.

"Thank you, Evan," she replied. "That means a lot to me. I wish you were here too. I could really use a hug right now."

"I'm sending you a virtual hug," Evan wrote back, "but I promise, one day soon, I'll give you a real one. I can't wait to hold you in my arms, Jillian. You deserve to be loved, and I'm going to make sure you know just how much I care about you."

Jillian felt tears welling up in her eyes as she read his words. It was everything she had ever wanted to hear, everything she had been yearning for. She knew that she was falling in love with Evan, and it scared her a little. But at the same time, it felt so right. She had been alone for so long, and now, here was this wonderful man who seemed to genuinely care about her, who was promising her the love and companionship she had been missing.

Their conversations continued to deepen, and Evan began to talk more about his life in the military. He described the challenges of being stationed in a war zone, the danger that was a constant part of his reality, and the stress of being so far away from home. He told her about his team, the men he considered brothers, and the close calls they had experienced together. Jillian couldn't help but worry about him, knowing that his life was constantly at risk.

"I just want you to stay safe," she told him one night. "I can't bear the thought of something happening to you."

Evan reassured her, telling her that he was careful and that he had been trained to handle the dangers of his job. But he also admitted that it was difficult, that there were times when he felt overwhelmed by the pressure and the responsibility. Jillian listened, offering him the same kind of support and understanding that he had given her.

As the weeks went by, Evan began to share more details about his personal life. He told Jillian about his financial situation, explaining that it was complicated because of his deployment. He mentioned that his accounts were frozen due to security protocols, and that it made things difficult for him. Jillian sympathized, understanding that his job came with unique challenges. She appreciated his openness, feeling that it only brought them closer together.

Then, one day, Evan asked her for a favor.

"Jillian, I hate to ask you this, but I'm in a bit of a bind. I need to send some money back home to take care of a few things, but with my accounts frozen, I can't access my funds. I've been racking my brain trying to figure out a solution, and I was wondering if you could help me out? It would just be a temporary loan, and I'd pay you back as soon as I'm able to access my accounts."

Jillian's heart skipped a beat. She was taken aback by his request, not because she didn't trust him, but because she hadn't expected it. She had never lent money to someone she hadn't met in person before, and the thought made her a little nervous. But at the same time, she trusted Evan. He had been nothing but kind and supportive, and she couldn't imagine that he would deceive her.

"I don't know, Evan," she replied hesitantly. "It's not that I don't want to help you, but I've never done something like this before. It makes me a little uneasy."

Evan quickly responded, reassuring her.

"I completely understand, Jillian. I wouldn't ask if it wasn't important, and I hate that I'm even in this position. But please know that I would never do anything to hurt you. You mean too much to me. If you're not comfortable, I'll figure something else out. I just thought I'd ask because I trust you more than anyone else."

Jillian felt a pang of guilt. Here was this man who had been so open and honest with her, who had made her feel loved and cared for, and now he was asking for her help. She didn't want to let him down, especially after everything he had done for her emotionally. But the voice in the back of her mind, the one that whispered doubts, grew louder.

"Let me think about it, okay?" she finally said. "I just need some time to process this."

"Of course, take all the time you need," Evan replied. "I don't want to pressure you. Just know that whatever you decide, I'm here for you, and I care about you more than you can imagine."

That night, Jillian couldn't sleep. Her mind was racing with thoughts and emotions. She kept replaying their conversations in her head, trying to make sense of everything. On one hand, she felt that she had finally found someone who truly understood her, who made her feel valued and loved. On the other hand, she couldn't shake the feeling that something wasn't quite right.

In the end, her desire to help Evan won out. She convinced herself that it was just a small loan, that he would pay her back as soon as he could. She couldn't bear the thought of him struggling while she had the means to help. The next day, she sent him the money, hoping that it would be the end of his troubles.

Evan was grateful, showering her with even more affection and promises of a future together. He told her that he couldn't wait to come home, to start a life with her, and to make all of their dreams come true. Jillian felt a mix of excitement and anxiety, but she pushed her doubts aside, telling herself that she was doing the right thing.

Little did she know, this was just the first step in a much larger scheme, one that would slowly unravel her life and leave her with nothing. But for now, Jillian was content, believing that she had found the perfect gentleman, the man who would finally make her happy.

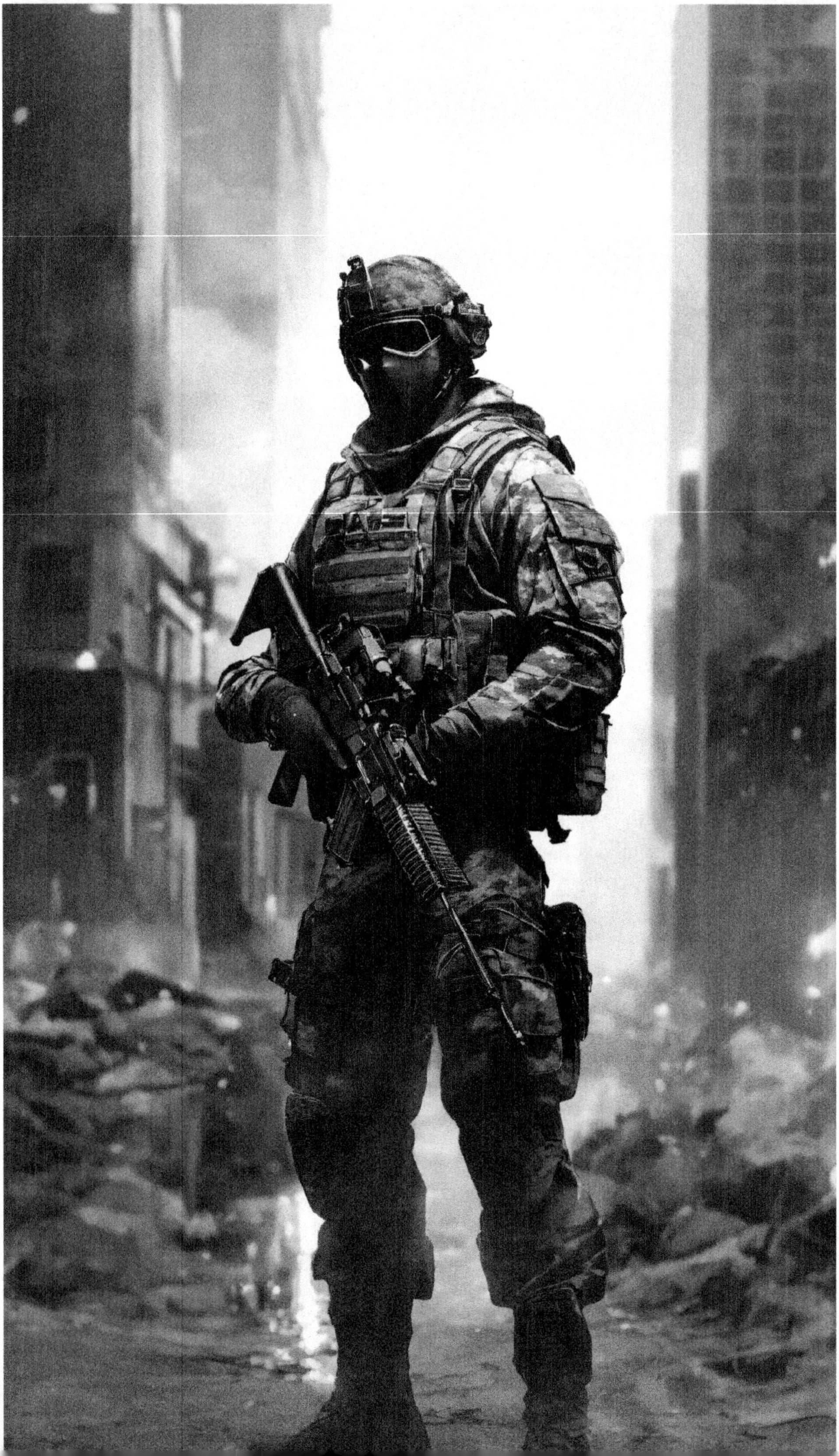

Chapter Three

The Web of Lies

As the days passed, Jillian found herself more and more entangled in her relationship with Evan. Their conversations became the highlight of her day. Whether it was during her lunch break, after her kids had gone to bed, or even in the few quiet moments she had in between her hectic schedule, she was always thinking about him. Evan seemed to have an uncanny ability to know exactly what to say to make her feel special, loved, and needed.

But Evan's requests for financial help began to increase. First, it was the small loan she had already sent him. He was profusely thankful and assured her it was just a temporary setback. A few days later, however, he came to her with another problem. His situation overseas had become more complicated, he explained, and he needed her assistance again. He talked about an urgent medical expense for a fellow soldier, a man who had saved his life during an ambush and who now desperately needed surgery. Evan's accounts were still frozen, and the military's bureaucracy was making it impossible for him to access his money.

Jillian hesitated. This was a much larger sum than before, and the urgency in his messages left her feeling anxious. She didn't know what to do. The story he told her was so detailed, so believable, that she couldn't bring herself to doubt him. And yet, there was a nagging voice in the back of her mind that questioned why he couldn't find another way to get the money. She considered talking to her friends or her kids about it, but she quickly dismissed the idea. They didn't know Evan like she did. They wouldn't understand.

"Evan, I really want to help you, but this is a lot of money," she typed, her fingers trembling slightly as she sent the message. "I'm not sure I can do this."

Evan's response was immediate and filled with emotion.

"Jillian, I wouldn't ask if I wasn't desperate. This man saved my life—he's like a brother to me. I feel so helpless not being able to do anything for him. You're the only person I can turn to. I promise I'll pay you back as soon as I get home. You mean the world to me, and I hate putting you in this position, but I don't know what else to do."

His words tugged at her heartstrings. The image of a brave soldier lying in a hospital bed, relying on her to make it through, was too much for her to bear. Jillian's empathy and compassion for Evan overrode her better judgment. She convinced herself that she couldn't let him down, that this was what you did for someone you loved.

She wired the money to the account he provided, all the while trying to ignore the small voice in her head that told her something was off. Evan's gratitude was overwhelming. He showered her with affection, telling her that he couldn't wait to come home and start their life together. He painted a picture of their future—weekends spent at the beach, cozy nights by the fire, and the love and laughter they would share. It was everything Jillian had ever wanted, and she allowed herself to believe in it, to see it as something real and attainable.

But as time went on, the requests from Evan didn't stop. They became more frequent, more urgent, and increasingly complicated. There was always another problem, another crisis that required Jillian's financial assistance. His accounts were still frozen, the military bureaucracy still impenetrable, and now there were legal fees, medical bills, and even ransom money to deal with. Evan's life seemed to be a never-ending string of disasters, and Jillian found herself increasingly anxious and overwhelmed.

Her bank account was slowly being drained, and the stress of trying to keep up with Evan's demands was taking its toll. She was losing sleep, barely eating, and found it difficult to focus at work. Her colleagues noticed that she seemed distracted, but she brushed off their concerns, insisting that everything was fine. She couldn't tell them what was really going on—she was too ashamed, too afraid of what they might say.

At home, her children began to notice the changes in her behavior as well. Jillian had always been a hands-on, attentive mother, but now she seemed distant, preoccupied. She would snap at them over small things, something she rarely did before, and often retreated to her bedroom to talk to Evan in private. Her daughter, Emma, who was 17, became particularly worried.

"Mom, is everything okay?" Emma asked one evening, after Jillian had spent hours on the phone with Evan, pacing the living room with a look of deep concern on her face.

Jillian forced a smile, trying to reassure her daughter. "I'm fine, sweetie. Just dealing with some stuff from work."

But Emma wasn't convinced. She had seen the stress in her mother's eyes, the way she seemed to be constantly on edge. She decided to keep a closer eye on her mom, worried that something was seriously wrong.

As the weeks turned into months, Jillian's life began to unravel. She was sending more and more money to Evan, often dipping into her savings and taking out loans to cover his demands. She was too deep in the situation to see it clearly, too emotionally invested to pull back. Every time she started to question what was happening, Evan would send her a heartfelt message, reminding her of his love and the future they were building together.

But the cracks were beginning to show. Jillian's finances were in shambles, and she was struggling to keep up with her bills. The stress was affecting her health, and she was constantly exhausted and on edge. Her relationships with her children and friends were suffering as well, as she became more isolated and secretive.

And still, Evan's requests continued. Each time, the stakes were higher, the stories more elaborate. Jillian felt like she was trapped in a nightmare, but she couldn't find a way out. She was in too deep, too committed to the idea that Evan was the love of her life, the man who would finally bring her happiness.

But little did she know, the web of lies that Evan had spun was about to come crashing down, and the truth would leave her devastated, with nothing left but shattered dreams and an empty bank account. The man she had trusted, the man she had loved, was not who he claimed to be, and Jillian was about to lose everything.

Chapter Four

The Unraveling

Jillian's life had become a whirlwind of confusion and stress. The love and warmth she once felt from Evan were overshadowed by the anxiety that gripped her daily. Each time her phone buzzed, her heart would leap into her throat. She knew it would be another message from Evan, and with each one, she felt the knot in her stomach tighten. She didn't know how much more she could take, but she also couldn't bring herself to walk away.

One evening, after yet another plea for help from Evan, Jillian sat down at her kitchen table, staring at the screen of her laptop. She had just wired him a substantial sum to cover what he claimed was a ransom for a fellow soldier who had been kidnapped. The amount was more than she could afford, but Evan had sounded desperate, and she couldn't bear the thought of letting him down. Still, something didn't sit right with her. The story seemed far-fetched, even for the chaotic life Evan described living overseas.

Jillian opened a new tab and started typing, her fingers trembling slightly. She began researching military protocols, curious about how such situations would typically be handled. The more she read, the more uneasy she became. None of it matched up with what Evan had told her. There were procedures in place, emergency funds, and support systems that would prevent soldiers from being put in such dire situations. The inconsistencies were glaring, but Jillian couldn't fully process them. She was too emotionally invested in the idea of Evan, in the dream of the life they would share once he returned home.

Her thoughts were interrupted by a knock on the front door. Startled, Jillian got up and walked to the door, opening it to find her friend and colleague, Sarah, standing on the porch. Sarah had been one of the few people who noticed the changes in Jillian over the past few months, and she had grown increasingly concerned.

"Hey, Jillian. Can I come in?" Sarah asked gently, her eyes filled with concern.

Jillian hesitated for a moment before stepping aside to let her in. "Sure, come on in."

Sarah walked into the living room and sat down on the couch, gesturing for Jillian to join her. "I've been worried about you. You've seemed so distant lately, and I just wanted to check in and see if everything's okay."

Jillian forced a smile, trying to appear as though everything was fine. "I'm just dealing with a lot right now. Work has been stressful, and there's... well, there's a lot going on."

Sarah nodded, but she didn't look convinced. "I get that, but it seems like more than just work. You know you can talk to me, right? Whatever it is, I'm here for you."

Jillian sighed, her defenses starting to crumble. She had been carrying the burden of her secret relationship with Evan for so long, and she hadn't realized how much it was weighing her down. The idea of confiding in someone, of sharing what she was going through, was both terrifying and liberating.

"There is something," Jillian admitted, her voice barely above a whisper. "But it's complicated."

Sarah reached out and took Jillian's hand, giving it a reassuring squeeze. "Whatever it is, you don't have to go through it alone. Just tell me what's going on."

Jillian hesitated, her mind racing. She didn't know where to start or how to explain everything that had happened. But as she looked into Sarah's kind eyes, she felt a wave of emotion wash over her. She couldn't keep this to herself any longer.

"I've been... I've been in a relationship," Jillian began, her voice shaking. "With someone I met online. His name is Evan, and he's a soldier stationed overseas. We've been talking for months, and I really thought he was the one. But now, I don't know what to think."

Sarah listened intently as Jillian recounted the story of how she had met Evan, how he had swept her off her feet with his charm and affection, and how he had gradually begun asking for money. She described the elaborate stories he told her, the financial demands that kept increasing, and the toll it was taking on her life. As Jillian spoke, Sarah's expression grew increasingly serious.

"Jillian," Sarah said carefully once she had finished, "I hate to say this, but it sounds like you might be involved in a scam."

The word hit Jillian like a punch to the gut. She recoiled, shaking her head in denial. "No, Evan wouldn't do that. He loves me. He's been through so much, and he just needs help."

"I know this is hard to hear," Sarah continued gently, "but I've read about situations like this. Scammers target people online, especially those looking for love, and they create these elaborate stories to manipulate them into sending money. It's called a 'romance scam.' They're really good at what they do, and they make it all seem so real."

Jillian's mind raced as she tried to process what Sarah was saying. The idea that Evan might not be who he claimed to be was too painful to accept. But at the same time, the doubts that had been nagging at her for weeks suddenly seemed to make sense. The inconsistencies, the constant crises, the never-ending requests for money—it all pointed to something she hadn't wanted to see.

"No... it can't be," Jillian whispered, tears welling up in her eyes. "What if you're wrong? What if he's really in trouble?"

"I hope I'm wrong," Sarah said softly. "But you need to protect yourself. Maybe we could look into it together, see if there's any way to verify his story. If he's real, then we'll find a way to help him that doesn't put you in financial jeopardy. But if he's not... you need to know that too."

Jillian felt a lump form in her throat. She didn't want to believe that the man she had fallen in love with could be a fraud. But the fear that Sarah might be right was too strong to ignore. The thought of losing everything, of being taken advantage of, was almost too much to bear.

"Okay," Jillian finally agreed, her voice trembling. "Let's look into it."

Sarah gave her a reassuring smile, though the concern in her eyes remained. "We'll figure this out together, Jillian. No matter what, you're not alone in this."

With Sarah's help, Jillian began to dig deeper into Evan's story, searching for any evidence that could confirm or disprove his identity. The more they uncovered, the more Jillian's world began to unravel. She found inconsistencies in the photos Evan had sent her, noticed that his stories often contradicted each other, and discovered that the bank accounts she had wired money to were located in countries far from any military base.

It became increasingly clear that Evan was not who he claimed to be. Jillian's heart broke as the truth came to light. The man she had fallen in love with, the man she had sacrificed so much for, was a fabrication. The realization left her devastated, feeling foolish and betrayed. She had been manipulated, and now she was left to pick up the pieces of her shattered life.

But as Jillian faced the harsh reality, she also found strength in the support of her friends and family. She knew that the road ahead would be difficult, but she was determined to reclaim her life and hold those responsible accountable. And while she had lost so much, she was not about to lose her dignity or her resolve to see justice served.

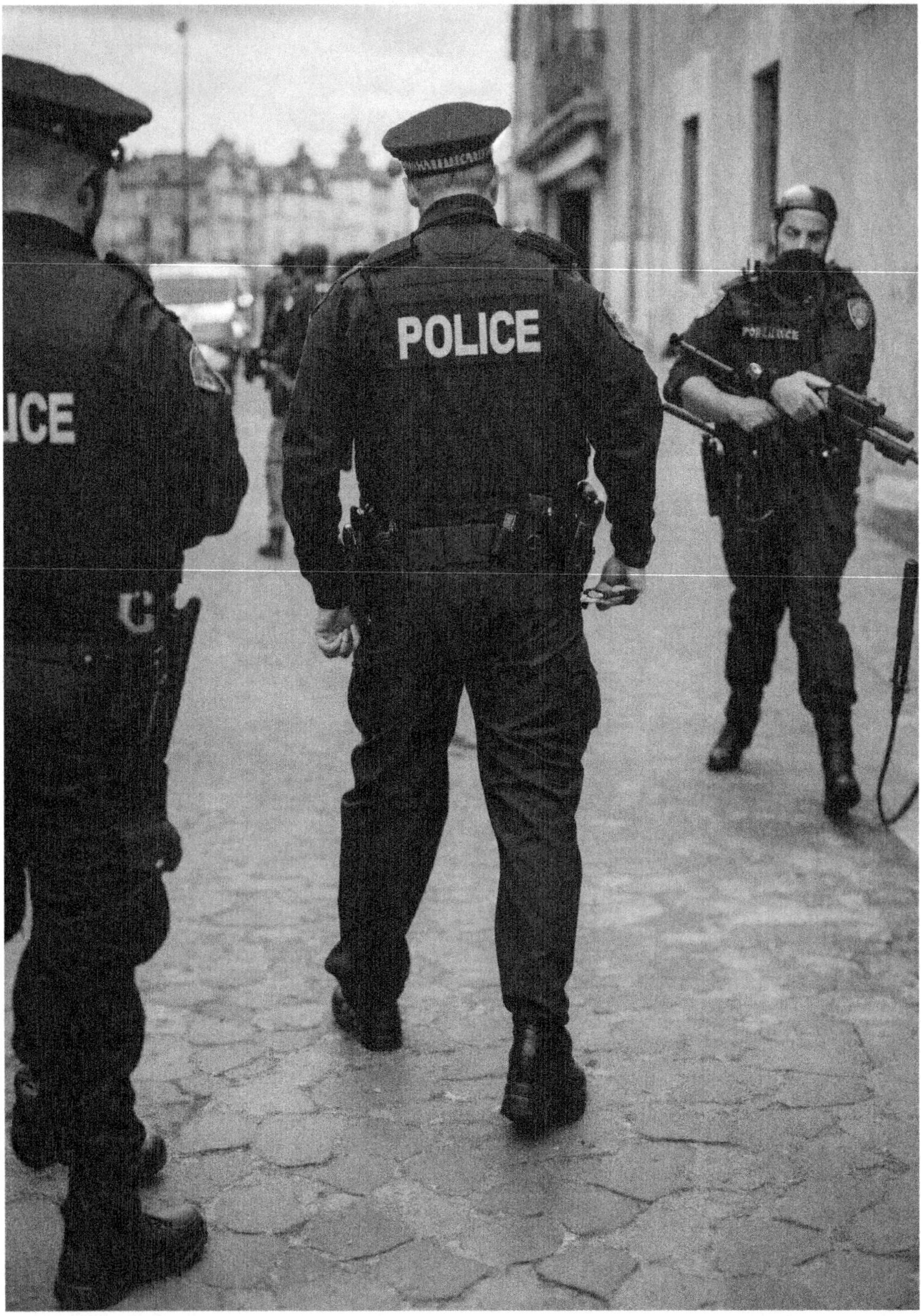

POLICE

Chapter Five

The Investigation Begins

The days following Jillian's heartbreaking revelation were some of the darkest she had ever faced. The reality of her situation weighed heavily on her, and the once-bright future she had envisioned with Evan seemed like a distant, cruel fantasy. But amidst the overwhelming sadness, a spark of determination began to grow within her. She wasn't just a victim—she was a mother, a professional, and a fighter. She knew she had to take action, not only for herself but for others who might be ensnared in similar scams.

Jillian's first step was to report the situation to the authorities. With Sarah's encouragement, she contacted her local police department and explained everything that had happened. The officers she spoke with were sympathetic and took her claims seriously. They informed her that romance scams were more common than she might think and assured her they would investigate her case.

But Jillian wasn't content to just wait for the police to act. She felt a deep sense of responsibility to uncover the truth, and she couldn't shake the nagging thought that there were others out there who were being deceived by the same people who had scammed her. Determined to find answers, Jillian began her own investigation.

She spent hours online, searching for any information that might link Evan to other victims. She joined forums and support groups for people who had been targeted by romance scams, sharing her story and learning from others who had gone through similar experiences. The stories she heard were eerily similar to her own, and it wasn't long before she started to see a pattern.

One night, as Jillian was scrolling through a support group forum, she came across a post that made her heart skip a beat. A woman named Denise had written about her experience with a man who called himself Evan Nicholson, a soldier stationed overseas. The details were almost identical to Jillian's story—the same romantic gestures, the same heartbreaking tales of hardship, and the same requests for money.

Jillian quickly messaged Denise, explaining that she had been in contact with a man using the same name and asking if they could talk. Denise responded almost immediately, and the two women soon found themselves on a video call, sharing their stories in real-time.

"I can't believe it," Denise said, her voice shaking with emotion. "It's like everything you're saying is exactly what happened to me. I thought I was the only one."

"So did I," Jillian replied, her heart heavy with empathy. "But it looks like this is bigger than either of us realized. We're dealing with professionals here."

As they compared notes, Jillian and Denise began to piece together the scam. They noticed that Evan's communication style was strikingly similar, as if he was reading from a script. Even the photos he had sent them were the same—images of a handsome, muscular man in military gear, smiling warmly into the camera. The realization that this man, or the person pretending to be him, was playing the same cruel game with multiple women only fueled Jillian's resolve.

"I think we need to go public with this," Jillian suggested. "If there are more of us out there, we need to warn them. Maybe if we share our stories, we can prevent this from happening to someone else."

Denise agreed, and the two women decided to take their story to the media. They reached out to a local news station, who were immediately interested in their story. The station arranged for an interview, and within days, Jillian and Denise found themselves sitting in a brightly lit studio, sharing their experience on live television.

The interview was both terrifying and cathartic for Jillian. She spoke candidly about how she had been drawn in by Evan's charm and how her emotions had clouded her judgment. She talked about the shame she had felt when she realized she had been scammed, and how she had almost let that shame keep her from speaking out. But as she looked into the camera, she knew that telling her story was the right thing to do.

"This isn't just about me," Jillian said, her voice steady with determination. "It's about all the people who are vulnerable to these kinds of scams. We need to raise awareness, and we need to hold these criminals accountable."

The response to the interview was overwhelming. Within hours, the news station was flooded with calls and emails from viewers who had either experienced similar scams or knew someone who had. Jillian and Denise were contacted by several other women who had been targeted by a man claiming to be Evan Nicholson. The realization that they were not alone, and that their efforts might be making a difference, gave Jillian a renewed sense of purpose.

But the media attention also attracted the interest of law enforcement agencies beyond her local police department. The FBI soon became involved, recognizing the scam as part of a larger, more sophisticated network that targeted vulnerable individuals across the country. Jillian was contacted by an FBI agent named Agent Cooper, who had been investigating similar cases for years.

"Ms. Wilson, I want you to know that we're taking this very seriously," Agent Cooper said during their first phone call. "These scammers are part of a well-organized criminal enterprise, and we're doing everything we can to track them down. Your willingness to come forward and share your story has been incredibly helpful in our investigation."

Jillian felt a mixture of relief and apprehension. She was glad to know that the authorities were taking action, but the thought of being involved in a federal investigation was daunting. Still, she knew that this was the right path, and she was willing to do whatever it took to bring the scammers to justice.

As the investigation progressed, Jillian found herself becoming more involved. She provided the FBI with every piece of evidence she had—emails, text messages, wire transfer receipts—anything that might help them track down the people behind the scam. She also continued to connect with other victims, offering support and encouragement as they navigated their own painful experiences.

Despite the challenges she faced, Jillian felt a growing sense of empowerment. She had gone from being a victim to being an advocate, using her voice to make a difference. And while the road ahead was still uncertain, she was determined to see it through to the end.

Little did she know, the investigation was about to take a dramatic turn—one that would bring her closer to the truth than she had ever imagined, and one that would ultimately lead to the downfall of the criminals who had taken so much from her.

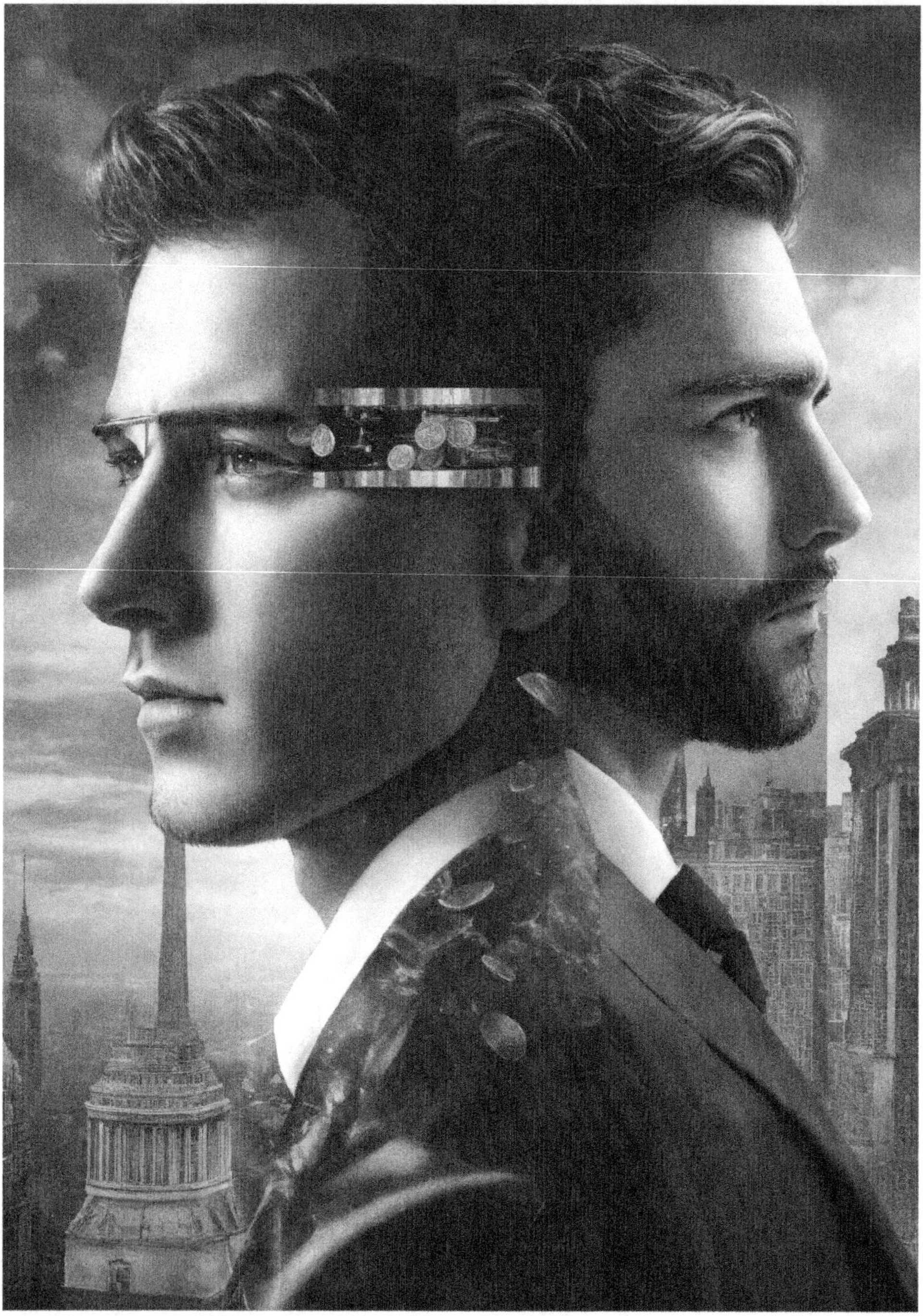

Chapter Six

The Web Unravels

As the FBI investigation intensified, Jillian found herself in the midst of a whirlwind of activity. Agent Cooper kept her updated on the progress, though much of what was happening was shrouded in secrecy. However, what he did share only deepened her understanding of the scale of the operation that had ensnared her.

The FBI had uncovered that the scammers operated out of several countries, utilizing a complex network of fake identities, stolen images, and scripted messages to prey on lonely and vulnerable individuals. The operation was highly organized, with different members of the group responsible for different aspects of the scam—some posed as the romantic leads, while others handled the financial transactions, and still others worked to cover their digital tracks.

Jillian learned that Evan Nicholson wasn't a real person, but rather a fabricated identity created using photos stolen from a real soldier's social media account. The man in the photos was unaware that his likeness was being used to deceive countless women around the world.

The knowledge that even the image she had fallen for was a lie stung deeply, but it also fueled her determination to see justice served.

One evening, as Jillian was going through her emails, she received a message from Agent Cooper that made her heart race. The subject line read: **"Urgent: Need Your Assistance."**

She opened the email to find a brief, but direct message:

"Jillian, we've made significant progress in the investigation. However, we need your help with something important. Please call me as soon as you can."

Without hesitation, Jillian picked up her phone and dialed Agent Cooper's number. He answered almost immediately, his voice calm but with an underlying urgency.

"Jillian, I'm glad you called. We've managed to track down one of the key figures in the scam—someone who has been coordinating a lot of the communication and financial transfers. We believe this person has information that could lead us to the rest of the group."

Jillian's pulse quickened. "That's incredible news, Agent Cooper. How can I help?"

"We need you to continue communicating with Evan," Agent Cooper explained. "We believe that with your help, we can gather more information to bring this operation down. I know it's a lot to ask, but you're in a unique position to assist us."

The idea of continuing to interact with the person who had deceived her was unsettling, but Jillian understood the importance of what the FBI was asking. She took a deep breath, steeling herself for what lay ahead.

"I'll do it," she said, her voice resolute. "Tell me what I need to do."

Over the next few days, Jillian resumed her online conversations with "Evan," carefully following the guidance provided by Agent Cooper. It was emotionally taxing to feign interest and affection for someone she now knew was a fraud, but she reminded herself that this was all in service of a greater goal.

As they exchanged messages, Jillian noticed subtle changes in Evan's behavior. He was more cautious, less forthcoming with details than he had been before. It was clear that he—or rather, the person behind the persona—sensed that something was different. But with Agent Cooper's help, Jillian was able to navigate the interactions without raising too much suspicion.

Then, one evening, Evan made a request that sent a chill down Jillian's spine. He asked her to transfer a large sum of money to a new account—one that was different from the one she had previously used. This was the break the FBI had been waiting for. Jillian immediately relayed the information to Agent Cooper, who assured her that they were close to making their move.

The following day, Jillian was at work when she received a call from Agent Cooper. His tone was more serious than usual, and Jillian could sense the gravity of the situation.

"Jillian, we've traced the new account to a location in Lagos, Nigeria," Agent Cooper said. "We believe it's connected to the individual we've been tracking. We're coordinating with local authorities to conduct a raid, but we need you to keep Evan engaged until we give the signal."

Jillian's heart pounded as she processed the information. This was it—the moment they had been working toward for weeks. She knew that the success of the operation depended on her ability to keep "Evan" distracted and unsuspecting.

With her nerves on edge, Jillian continued her conversation with Evan, doing her best to appear calm and interested. She asked him questions about his supposed life in the military, listened as he told her more fabricated stories, and even expressed concern about the hardships he claimed to be facing. All the while, she was acutely aware that this interaction could be one of the last before the operation came to a head.

As the minutes ticked by, Jillian's anxiety grew. She kept glancing at her phone, waiting for any word from Agent Cooper. Finally, after what felt like an eternity, her phone buzzed with a new message: **"It's done. They're in custody."**

Relief washed over Jillian as she read the words. The scammers had been caught. The people who had deceived her and so many others were finally facing justice. She quickly excused herself from the conversation with Evan, knowing that it would be the last time she would ever have to interact with him.

Later that evening, Jillian received a detailed update from Agent Cooper. The raid in Lagos had been successful, resulting in the arrest of several individuals connected to the scam. They had confiscated computers, phones, and other equipment that the scammers had used to perpetrate their crimes. The evidence gathered was expected to lead to even more arrests in the coming days.

For Jillian, the news was both a victory and a bittersweet moment. She had helped to bring down the people who had taken so much from her, but the emotional toll of the experience lingered. She knew that she would never get back the money she had lost, nor could she erase the pain of betrayal. But she also knew that she had played a crucial role in preventing others from falling into the same trap.

As she sat in her living room that night, reflecting on everything that had happened, Jillian felt a sense of closure. The web of deceit had been unraveled, and while the scars would remain, she was no longer a victim. She was a survivor, and her story was far from over.

Chapter Seven

The Fallout

Episode 7: The Fallout

With the scammers now in custody, Jillian expected to feel a sense of relief, but instead, she was overwhelmed by a mix of emotions. The immediate threat was gone, but the aftermath of the scam lingered, casting a long shadow over her life. The realization that the person she had trusted with her deepest emotions had been a complete fabrication was something she struggled to come to terms with.

In the days following the arrests, Jillian was contacted by the FBI several times. Agent Cooper and his team needed her to provide testimony and additional details about her interactions with the scammers. They assured her that her cooperation was vital to ensuring the culprits faced the full weight of the law. While Jillian was more than willing to help, each interview reopened wounds that had barely begun to heal.

The financial fallout from the scam was devastating. Jillian had drained her savings and even taken out loans to send money to "Evan." Now, with the realization that all of it was gone, she faced the harsh reality of her situation. The stress of the financial burden weighed heavily on her, as she struggled to keep up with her bills and provide for her children.

One evening, as Jillian sat at her kitchen table, going through a stack of unpaid bills, the enormity of her losses hit her. She had lost over $50,000 to the scam—money she had worked hard to save over the years. But the financial loss was only part of the story. The emotional toll of the scam was equally profound. Jillian had opened her heart to someone she believed was genuine, only to discover that it was all a lie.

As the weeks passed, the strain of the situation began to take a toll on Jillian's mental health. She found herself feeling anxious, depressed, and unable to sleep. The thought of the scam replayed in her mind constantly, and she struggled to focus on her work and her responsibilities as a mother. The once vibrant and optimistic woman was now a shadow of her former self, consumed by guilt and self-doubt.

Her relationships with friends and family also began to suffer. Jillian was too ashamed to tell most people what had happened, fearing that they would judge her for being so easily deceived. She withdrew from social activities, isolating herself in her home. The loneliness that had driven her to seek companionship online in the first place now returned with a vengeance, more intense than ever.

One day, Jillian received a call from her bank, informing her that her account was overdrawn. She had missed a payment on her mortgage, and the bank was threatening to foreclose on her home if she didn't catch up on her payments. Panic set in as Jillian realized that she was on the brink of losing everything she had worked so hard to build.

Desperate for a way out, Jillian considered selling her house and moving into a smaller, more affordable place. But the thought of uprooting her children from their home, where they had grown up and made so many memories, was heartbreaking. She couldn't bear the idea of adding more instability to their lives, especially after everything they had already been through.

Jillian knew she needed help, but she was too embarrassed to reach out to her friends or family. Instead, she began researching support groups for victims of online scams. She discovered that there were many others who had gone through similar experiences—people who had lost their life savings, their homes, and even their sense of self-worth. Reading their stories gave Jillian a sense of comfort, knowing that she wasn't alone in her struggle.

One evening, after putting her children to bed, Jillian sat down at her computer and joined an online support group for scam victims. As she read through the messages from other members, she felt a sense of camaraderie that she hadn't experienced in a long time. These were people who understood her pain, who had been through the same emotional rollercoaster and come out the other side.

After spending some time in the group, Jillian decided to share her own story. She described how she had met "Evan," how he had won her trust, and how she had been manipulated into sending him money. She also talked about the aftermath of the scam—the financial ruin, the emotional devastation, and the toll it had taken on her mental health.

As Jillian wrote, she felt a weight lifting off her shoulders. For the first time since the scam had been exposed, she was able to express her feelings openly, without fear of judgment. The support group members responded with words of encouragement and understanding, assuring her that she wasn't to blame for what had happened.

Over the next few weeks, Jillian continued to participate in the support group, finding solace in the shared experiences of others. She began to realize that while the scam had taken so much from her, it didn't have to define her future. She started to focus on rebuilding her life, one step at a time.

With the help of the support group, Jillian began to take control of her finances. She worked with a financial advisor to create a budget and a plan to pay off her debts. She also started attending therapy sessions to address the emotional trauma she had experienced. Slowly but surely, she began to regain her sense of self-worth and confidence.

But the journey was far from easy. There were days when Jillian felt overwhelmed by the enormity of what she had lost, when the guilt and shame threatened to pull her back into a dark place. But each time, she reminded herself that she was a survivor, not a victim. She had faced the worst and come out stronger on the other side.

As Jillian continued to rebuild her life, she also became determined to help others avoid falling into the same trap. She started speaking out about her experience, sharing her story with local news outlets and community groups. She wanted to raise awareness about online scams and educate others on how to protect themselves from being deceived.

Jillian's efforts didn't go unnoticed. She was invited to speak at a national conference on online fraud, where she shared the stage with cybersecurity experts and law enforcement officials. Her story resonated with many in the audience, and she received numerous messages of thanks from people who had been touched by her courage.

By the time the conference ended, Jillian realized that she had found a new purpose. She was no longer the woman who had been scammed—she was an advocate, a fighter, and a beacon of hope for others who had been through similar experiences. And while the pain of what had happened would never completely disappear, Jillian knew that she had the strength to face whatever challenges lay ahead.

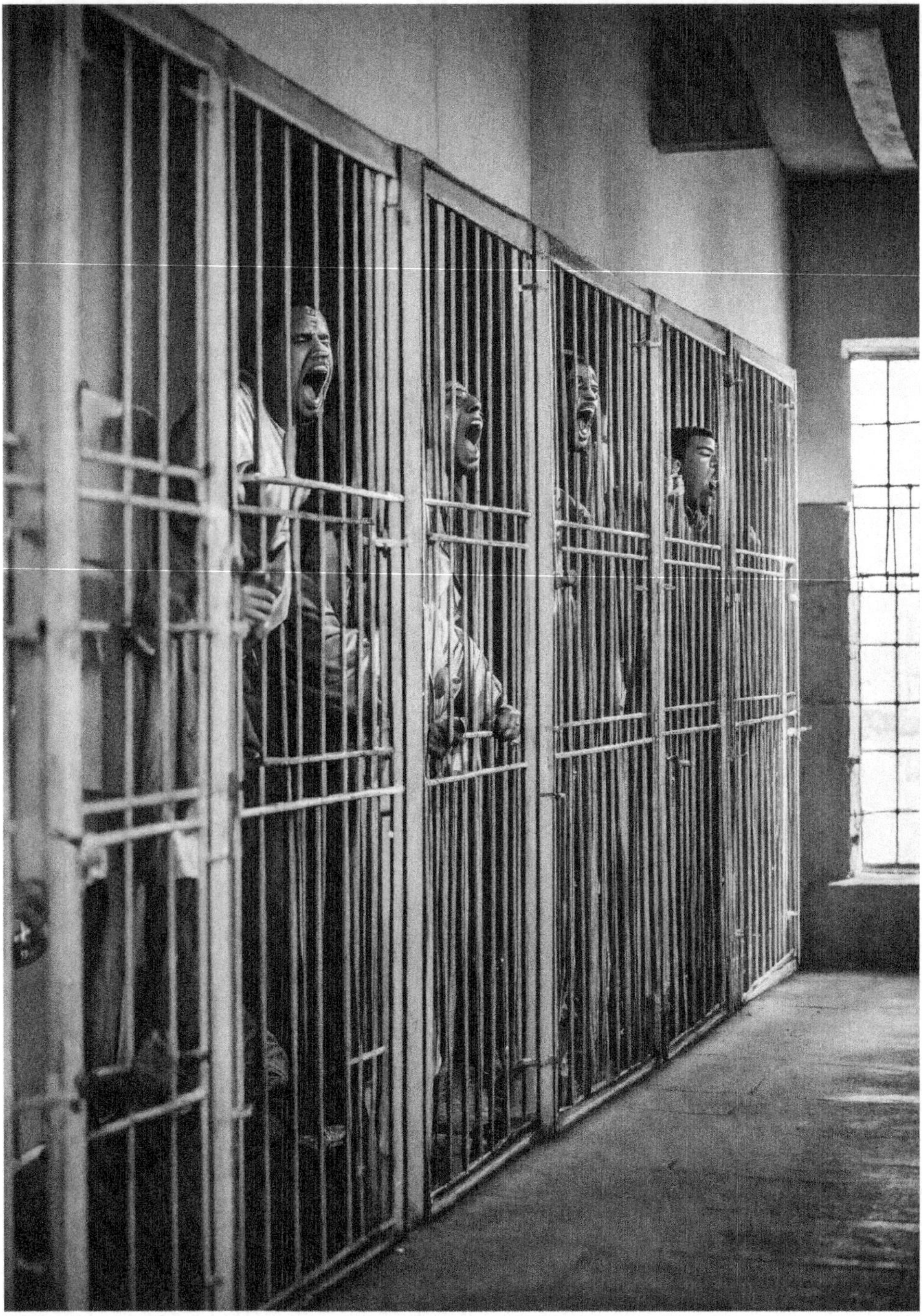

Chapter Eight

The Legal Battle

As Jillian continued her journey toward healing, the legal process against the scammers who had targeted her moved forward. The FBI and the Department of Justice were building a solid case against the network of criminals involved in the scheme. They informed Jillian that she might need to testify in court, recounting her experience to help ensure that those responsible would face justice.

The thought of confronting the scammers in court filled Jillian with a mix of dread and determination. She knew that her testimony could be crucial in securing a conviction, but the idea of reliving the trauma in front of a courtroom full of strangers was terrifying. Despite her fears, Jillian resolved to see the process through. She had already lost so much—her savings, her sense of security, and a significant portion of her self-esteem. She was determined to do everything she could to prevent others from falling victim to the same scam.

In preparation for the trial, Jillian met with the prosecuting attorney, Jessica Palmer, a sharp and compassionate lawyer who specialized in fraud cases. Jessica assured Jillian that she would be there to support her every step of the way. Together, they went over the details of Jillian's interactions with "Evan" and the financial transactions she had made. Jessica explained how the scammers had used sophisticated techniques to create a believable persona and manipulate Jillian into trusting them.

As the trial date approached, Jillian's anxiety intensified. She found herself constantly replaying the events of the scam in her mind, questioning her decisions, and wondering how she could have been so blind to the deception. But with the support of her therapist, her support group, and her children, Jillian was able to keep moving forward. She reminded herself that the scam had been designed to exploit her vulnerabilities, and that the blame lay with the criminals, not with her.

The day of the trial finally arrived. Jillian sat in the courtroom, her heart pounding as she watched the defendants being led in. There were three of them: two men and one woman, all part of the international scam network that had ensnared her. They appeared calm and composed, a stark contrast to the turmoil Jillian felt inside. But she reminded herself that their calm demeanor was just another layer of their deception—a facade they had perfected over years of exploiting others.

When it was Jillian's turn to take the stand, she felt a wave of nausea wash over her. The courtroom seemed to blur around her as she made her way to the witness box. But as she sat down and took a deep breath, she felt a sense of resolve settle over her. She had come this far, and she wasn't going to let fear stop her now.

Jessica began by asking Jillian to describe how she had met "Evan" and the nature of their relationship. Jillian spoke clearly and steadily, recounting the early days of their communication, the affection and attention "Evan" had shown her, and how he had gradually introduced the idea of needing money for various emergencies. As she spoke, Jillian could feel the eyes of the courtroom on her, but she focused on Jessica's calm and reassuring presence.

The defense attorney tried to undermine Jillian's credibility, suggesting that she had been careless or even complicit in the scam. But Jillian held her ground, explaining how the scammers had manipulated her emotions and used her desire for love and companionship against her. Jessica stepped in to redirect the questioning, emphasizing the sophisticated nature of the scam and how it had been designed to deceive even the most cautious individuals.

As the cross-examination continued, Jillian found herself growing more confident. She realized that by sharing her story, she was not only helping to bring the scammers to justice but also reclaiming her own narrative. She was no longer a passive victim; she was an active participant in the fight against the criminals who had wronged her.

When the trial finally concluded, the jury deliberated for several hours before returning with a verdict. The scammers were found guilty on multiple counts of fraud, conspiracy, and money laundering. The judge sentenced them to lengthy prison terms, ensuring that they would not be able to prey on others for a long time.

As Jillian left the courtroom, she felt a sense of closure that had eluded her since the scam had first been uncovered. The legal battle had been exhausting, but it had also been empowering. Jillian had faced her fears, stood up to those who had wronged her, and emerged stronger on the other side.

But while the verdict brought some measure of justice, Jillian knew that the scars from the scam would take time to heal. The financial losses would take years to recover, and the emotional wounds would require continued care and attention. However, the trial had given her a renewed sense of purpose. She had helped to stop a group of criminals and had made a difference in the lives of others who might have been targeted.

In the weeks following the trial, Jillian continued her work with the support group, now taking on a more active role in helping others navigate the aftermath of scams. She also began volunteering with organizations dedicated to educating the public about online fraud, sharing her story as a cautionary tale and offering advice on how to avoid falling into similar traps.

Jillian's life was far from perfect, and the road ahead was still challenging. But she was no longer defined by the scam. She was a survivor, a fighter, and an advocate. And while she had lost so much, she had also gained something invaluable: the knowledge that she had the strength to overcome even the darkest of times and to help others do the same.

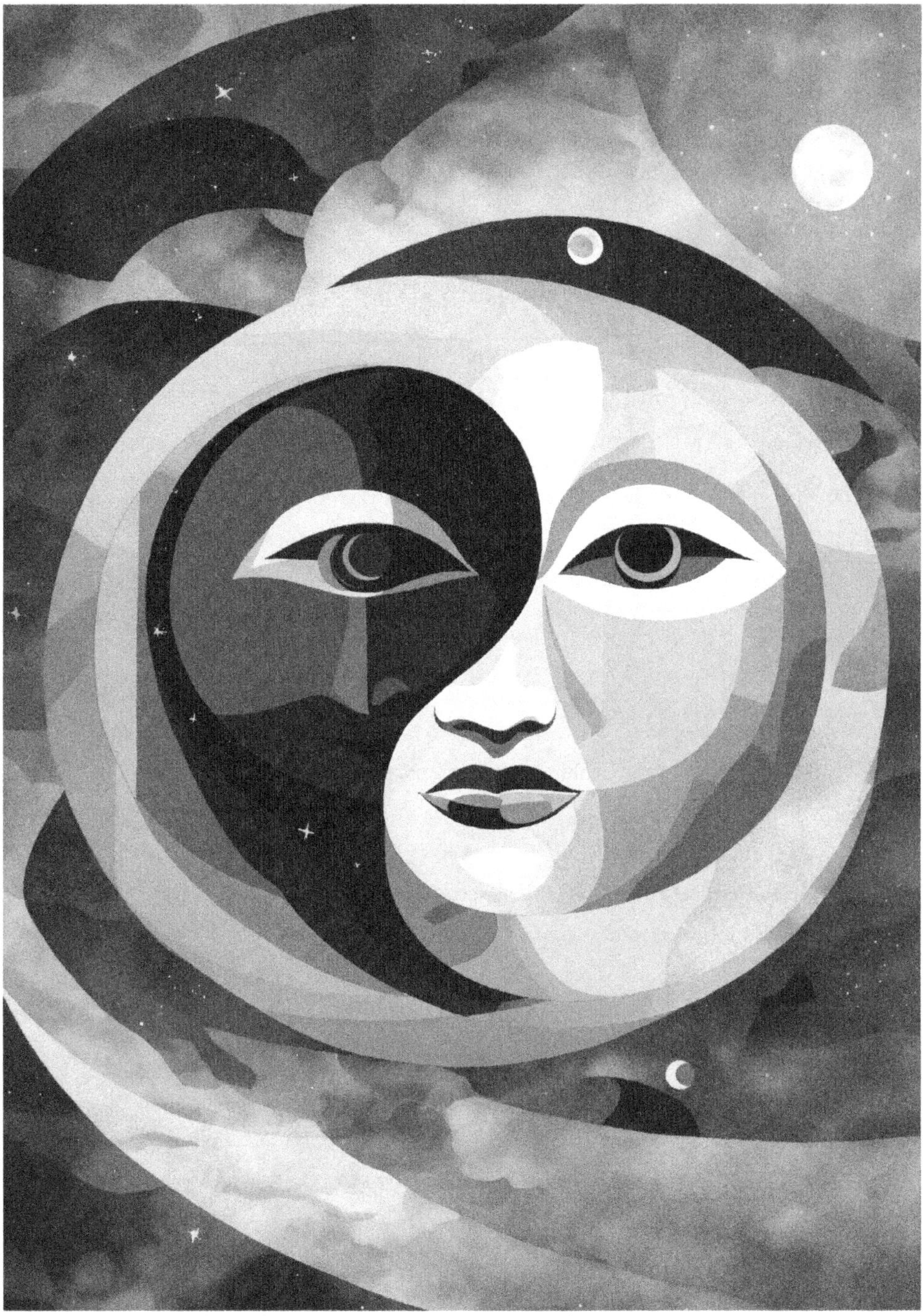

Chapter Nine

A New Beginning

With the trial behind her and a measure of justice served, Jillian was left to navigate the next chapter of her life. The aftermath of the scam had left her emotionally and financially drained, but she was determined to rebuild. She knew that starting over wouldn't be easy, but she was resolved to find a path forward.

Jillian's first step was to address her financial situation. The loss of her savings and the mounting debt had taken a heavy toll. She consulted a financial advisor to help her create a plan for recovery. The advisor recommended a strict budget, prioritizing essential expenses and exploring options for debt relief. Jillian was committed to following the plan, even though it meant making significant lifestyle changes and cutting back on many of the comforts she had once enjoyed.

In addition to managing her finances, Jillian focused on her emotional well-being. She continued attending therapy sessions to work through the trauma of the scam and to rebuild her self-esteem. Her therapist encouraged her to practice self-care and to set small, achievable goals for herself. Jillian found solace in activities she had once enjoyed but had neglected during the turmoil of the scam, such as painting and gardening. These hobbies provided her with a sense of accomplishment and a welcome distraction from her worries.

Her children, who had been incredibly supportive throughout the ordeal, continued to be a source of strength. Jillian's relationship with them grew even stronger as they navigated this challenging period together. Her teenagers admired her resilience and often pitched in to help with household responsibilities, demonstrating their maturity and understanding.

As Jillian worked on rebuilding her life, she also began to consider new opportunities for herself. The experience of the scam had given her a newfound sense of purpose, and she wanted to use her experience to make a positive impact. She explored various volunteer opportunities and eventually decided to focus on advocacy and education related to online fraud. Her story and her insights could help others avoid falling victim to similar scams.

Jillian joined a local organization dedicated to fraud prevention, where she became an active member of their outreach and education programs. She participated in workshops and seminars, sharing her story and providing practical advice on how to recognize and avoid scams. Her firsthand experience made her an effective advocate, and she was passionate about helping others stay informed and vigilant.

One of the highlights of Jillian's new role was speaking at community events and schools. She crafted her presentations to be engaging and informative, using real-life examples to illustrate the dangers of online fraud. Her personal story resonated with many, and she was often approached by individuals who shared their own experiences or sought advice on protecting themselves.

In addition to her work with the fraud prevention organization, Jillian also began to explore new career opportunities. She updated her resume and networked with professionals in her field. Although it was a challenging job market, Jillian remained optimistic and persistent. Her dedication and resilience were evident, and she eventually secured a position at a nonprofit organization focused on supporting victims of financial crime.

The new job was a perfect fit for Jillian. It allowed her to use her skills and experience to make a difference while providing a stable income. The work was fulfilling and aligned with her values, and she found great satisfaction in helping others navigate the challenges she had once faced herself.

Despite the progress Jillian was making, the road to recovery was not without its setbacks. There were moments when she felt overwhelmed by the weight of her past, and the financial strain continued to be a concern. But Jillian learned to manage her stress through mindfulness practices and leaned on her support network when she needed help.

As time went on, Jillian's life began to stabilize. She had rebuilt her financial footing, found meaningful work, and developed a renewed sense of purpose. Her involvement in fraud prevention advocacy allowed her to turn her pain into a powerful force for good. She was no longer a victim; she was a survivor and a beacon of hope for others facing similar challenges.

Jillian's journey was a testament to her strength and resilience. She had faced immense adversity and emerged stronger, more determined, and more compassionate. Her story was one of transformation—a story of finding light in the darkest of times and using that light to guide others toward a brighter future.

As she looked ahead, Jillian was hopeful and excited about the possibilities that lay before her. She knew that while the scars of her past would always be a part of her, they would no longer define her. Instead, she embraced her new role as an advocate and mentor, ready to continue making a positive impact and helping others find their own path to recovery and empowerment.

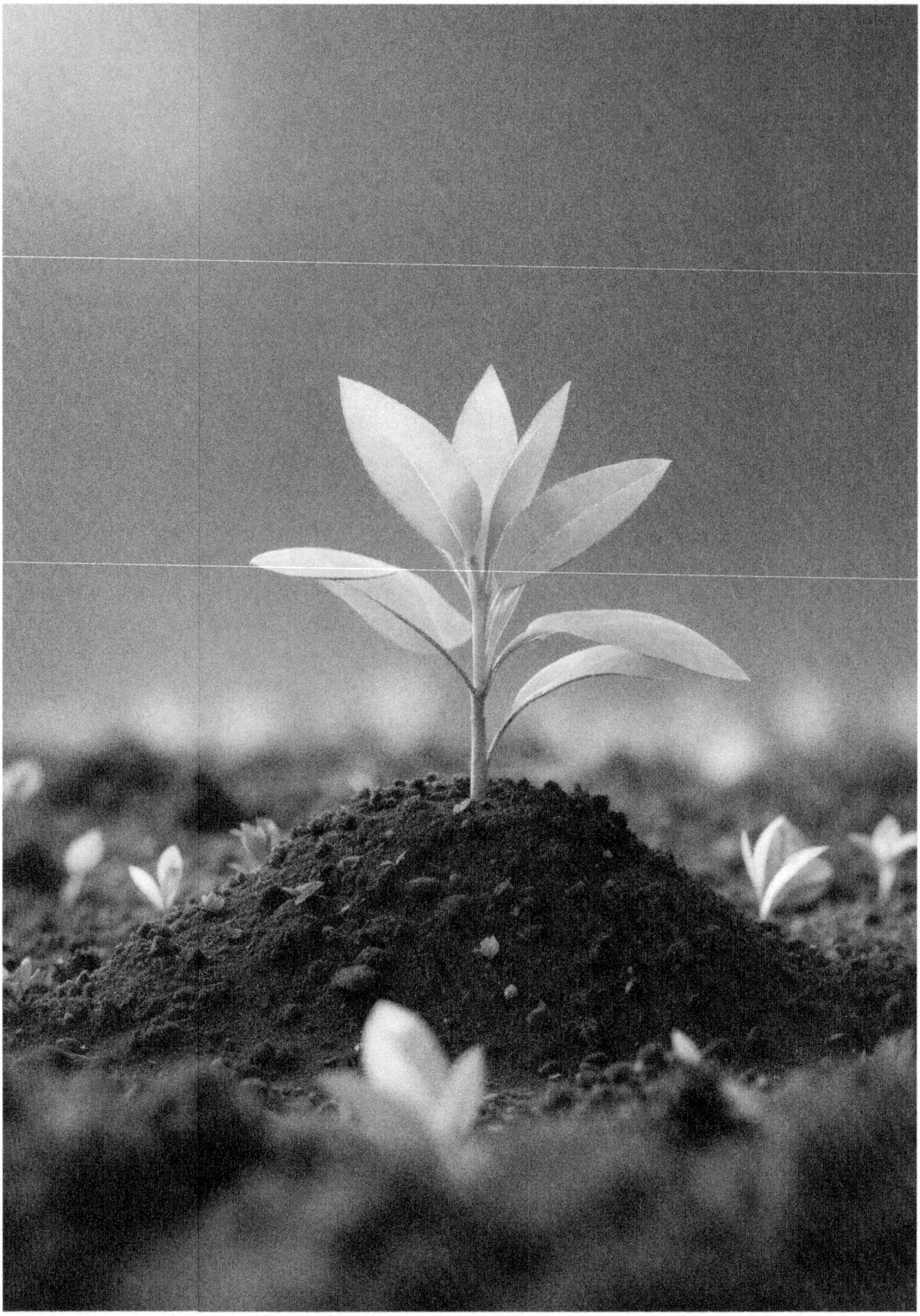

Chapter Ten

Moving Forward

Months had passed since Jillian's last public appearance as a fraud prevention advocate, and she had made significant strides in her personal and professional life. Her experiences had not only reshaped her understanding of online fraud but had also inspired her to make a lasting difference in the world.

Jillian's work with the nonprofit organization had expanded. She now led a team of volunteers dedicated to supporting victims of financial scams. Her leadership role allowed her to mentor others, guiding them through their own recovery processes and sharing her expertise to help them navigate the complexities of financial crime. Her firsthand experience made her an invaluable asset to the team, and her compassion and dedication shone through in all her interactions.

She continued to speak at community events and educational workshops, refining her presentations to be more impactful and accessible. Her story, once a source of deep personal pain, had become a powerful tool for raising awareness and empowering others. Jillian's ability to connect with her audience on a personal level made her a sought-after speaker, and she was invited to participate in various media appearances, including interviews and podcasts, to further spread her message.

In addition to her advocacy work, Jillian took on a new project: writing a book about her experiences. The book, tentatively titled "From Deception to Redemption: My Journey Through a Romance Scam," was a comprehensive account of her ordeal, offering readers insight into the psychological and emotional impact of such scams. It included practical advice on recognizing and avoiding fraud, as well as personal reflections on her path to recovery. The book was not only a means of healing for Jillian but also a valuable resource for others seeking to understand and protect themselves from similar dangers.

Writing the book was a cathartic process for Jillian. It allowed her to reflect on her journey and gain closure. She poured her heart into the manuscript, sharing the raw, honest details of her experience. The book also featured contributions from experts in fraud prevention, adding depth and credibility to her narrative.

As Jillian's professional life flourished, her personal life also began to take shape. She had made new friends through her advocacy work and reconnected with old acquaintances. Her relationships with her children remained strong, and they continued to support each other through life's ups and downs. Jillian found comfort in the stability and love of her family, which had been a constant source of strength throughout her recovery.

Jillian also took time for herself, engaging in activities that brought her joy and fulfillment. She traveled to new places, explored hobbies she had put on hold, and enjoyed quiet moments of reflection. These experiences helped her regain a sense of balance and well-being, reminding her of the importance of self-care and personal growth.

Despite her progress, Jillian remained vigilant about the risks of online scams. She continued to educate herself about emerging threats and worked closely with her organization to develop new strategies for fraud prevention. Her dedication to staying informed and proactive ensured that she could continue to provide valuable support and guidance to others.

One of the most rewarding aspects of Jillian's journey was seeing the positive impact of her work on others. She received countless messages of gratitude from individuals whose lives had been changed by her advocacy. Knowing that her efforts had helped others avoid or recover from scams brought her immense satisfaction and a sense of purpose.

As Jillian reflected on her journey, she felt a deep sense of pride in how far she had come. She had faced incredible challenges and emerged stronger, more resilient, and more compassionate. Her experiences had shaped her into a powerful advocate for change, and she was committed to continuing her work to make a difference.

Looking ahead, Jillian remained optimistic about the future. She was excited about the opportunities to expand her advocacy efforts, reach new audiences, and continue making a positive impact. She had learned valuable lessons about strength, resilience, and the importance of community support, and she was determined to use those lessons to help others navigate their own paths to recovery.

Jillian's story was a testament to the power of perseverance and the ability to turn adversity into a force for good. Her journey from victim to advocate was an inspiring example of how even the darkest experiences can lead to a brighter, more fulfilling future. As she moved forward, Jillian carried with her the knowledge that she had not only overcome her own challenges but had also paved the way for others to find hope and healing in their own lives.

Chapter Eleven

About the Author

Mike Nash is an accomplished author with a background in finance, having penned several books that offer insights into financial literacy and economic strategies. Known for his clear, accessible writing style, Mike has helped countless readers navigate the complexities of personal finance.

With *The Love Scam*, Mike ventures into new territory, combining his analytical skills with investigative journalism to explore the world of online romance scams. This book marks his first foray into investigative writing, shedding light on the emotional and financial dangers lurking in the digital dating landscape. Mike's passion for helping others protect their financial well-being continues to drive his work, now extending into the realm of personal safety in online relationships.

Printed in Great Britain
by Amazon